Fred Rogers
PRODUCTIONS

Donkey Hodie™

Donkey Hodie Helps an Elephant

adapted by **Tina Gallo**
based on the screenplay *"A Big Favor For Grampy"*
written by **Adam Rudman** and **David Rudman**

Ready-to-Read

Simon Spotlight
New York London Toronto Sydney New Delhi

SIMON SPOTLIGHT

An imprint of Simon & Schuster Children's Publishing Division

1230 Avenue of the Americas, New York, New York 10020

This Simon Spotlight edition December 2021

© 2021 The Fred Rogers Company.

Donkey Hodie is produced by Fred Rogers Productions and Spiffy Pictures.

All rights reserved, including the right of reproduction in whole or in part in any form.

SIMON SPOTLIGHT, READY-TO-READ, and colophon are registered trademarks of Simon & Schuster, Inc.

For information about special discounts for bulk purchases, please contact Simon & Schuster Special Sales at 1-866-506-1949 or business@simonandschuster.com.

Manufactured in the United States of America 1021 LAK

10 9 8 7 6 5 4 3 2 1

ISBN 978-1-5344-9941-6 (hc)

ISBN 978-1-5344-9940-9 (pbk)

ISBN 978-1-5344-9942-3 (ebook)

"Hi, Donkey Hodie," Grampy Hodie said. "Will you please walk my pet elephant, Gregory?"

Donkey was excited.
"I, Donkey Hodie, will take
Gregory for a walk!"
she said.

"Are you ready, Gregory?"
Donkey asked.

Gregory did not move.

"Think, Donkey Hodie, think!" Donkey said.

Just then, Purple Panda stopped by on his skateboard.

"Gregory will not move," Donkey told Panda.

Donkey looked at
the skateboard.
She had an idea!

She and Panda put Gregory on the skateboard.

The skateboard rolled away
with Gregory on it!

Donkey and Panda
stopped the skateboard,
and Gregory got off it.

"Sorry I could not help,
but I have to go now,"
Panda said.

"Can I help?"
Duck Duck asked.
"My book says elephants like
to eat peanuts. . . ."

Donkey put a huge peanut
on a fishing pole.
Gregory did not move.

Then Bob Dog said
Gregory might want
to fetch a ball.

Bob Dog threw the ball.
Gregory did not move.

The ball landed in a nest.
Donkey went to get it
and frowned.

Clyde the Cloud said, "You look upset, Donkey." "Gregory will not move," she said.

"When I feel upset,
I sing a little song,"
Clyde said.

"I just say, 'Stop! Stop!'
Take a breath,
breathe in deep down
to my tummy. . . ."

Then he sang,
"When I take a deep breath,
I blow my troubles away!"

Donkey took a deep breath.

She felt calm and ready
to solve her problem.

Back in the yard, Donkey
saw a radio with toys
that belonged to Gregory.
She had a new idea.

She turned on the radio,
and music played.
Gregory moved!

Gregory loved walking with music!

Donkey was so proud that she walked Gregory and helped Grampy!